Happy

neezy

Doc

Grumpy

GROLIER
BOOK CLUB EDITION

WALT DISNEY'S

Snow White
and the
Seven Dwarfs

**Random House
New York**

Copyright © 1973 by The Walt Disney Company. All rights reserved under
International and Pan-American Copyright Conventions. Published in the
United States by Random House, Inc., New York, and simultaneously in
Canada by Random House of Canada Limited, Toronto.

Library of Congress Cataloging in Publication Data
Main entry under title: Walt Disney's Snow White and the seven dwarfs.
(Disney's wonderful world of reading)
SUMMARY: A simplified retelling of the tale in which a fair princess, left to
die in the woods, is cared for by seven little men.
[1. Fairy tales. 2. Folklore] I. Snow White and the seven dwarfs.
[Motion picture]   II. Title   PZ8.C189Wal   398.2′2   72-12653
ISBN 0-394-82625-6   ISBN 0-394-92625-0 (lib. bdg.)

Manufactured in the United States of America

2 3 4   Q R S T

Long ago there lived a princess named
Snow White. She was a beautiful princess.
And like all princesses she lived in a castle.

Her stepmother, the queen,
also lived in the castle.
The queen had a magic mirror.
Every day she looked
into the mirror and
asked the same thing.

"Mirror, mirror on the wall. Who is the fairest
one of all?"

The mirror always gave her the same answer.
"Oh, queen, YOU are the fairest one of all."

But one day the mirror had a different answer. "Snow White is the fairest in the land," it said.

The proud queen became very angry. SHE wanted to be the most beautiful lady in the land.

The queen sent for the woodman.

"Take Snow White away," she told him.

"She must never come back to the castle. You must kill her."

The woodman took Snow White into the woods.

But he could not kill the sweet princess.

He loved her too much.

Instead, he said, "Run away, child—quickly!

You must hide from the queen. She wants to kill you."

Snow White ran through the woods as fast as
she could. It was very dark under the trees.
And she heard scary noises. But still she ran on.

At last Snow White could run no more. She fell
to the ground and cried herself to sleep.

Two rabbits hopped up to sit by Snow White.
A little bird flew down and sang to her.
Then two deer came to stand behind her.
And a raccoon and a turtle sat by her feet.

Snow White awoke and sat up.
She was not afraid any more.

The friendly animals led her along a little path.

Soon they came to a small house.

Snow White tapped at the door.

"Is anyone home?" she called.

The animals pushed open the door.
Snow White followed them into the house.

She saw a table
and seven little chairs.
There were also seven
little bowls.

"My goodness!" she said. "Seven little children
must live here. I wonder where they are?"

She went into the kitchen. What a mess!
There were dirty dishes everywhere.

"These are certainly seven messy little
children," she said.

"I think I will clean their house for them.
Then perhaps they will let me live here with them."

Snow White got down on her hands and knees and cleaned the floor.

Then she washed all the dirty dishes. The deer and the rabbit helped her.

When the cleaning-up was done, Snow White
and the animals went upstairs.

There she found seven little wooden beds.
Snow White lay down and soon fell
fast asleep.

Not far away, seven little men were climbing
out of a cave. They had been working there all day,
digging diamonds. Now it was time to go home.

As they walked through the woods, they sang:

"Hi-ho! Hi-ho!
It's home from work
we go!"

The seven dwarfs walked up to the
very house where Snow White was sleeping.

It was THEIR house.

"There's a light in our house!" said one.
"Somebody must be in there," said another.

They were a little scared.

Quietly, they crept into the house.

They looked all around.

"The floor is clean," said one of them.

"The dishes have been washed," said another.

"Who do you suppose did this?" asked a third.

One by one the dwarfs tiptoed up the stairs.
Perhaps somebody was hiding up there.

They pushed against the door.
Suddenly it opened, and the dwarfs
fell into the bedroom.

The noise woke up Snow White.
She sat up, her eyes wide open.

"Oh, my!" she said. "You are not children.
You are little men."

"That is right," said one of the dwarfs.
"But who are you?"

"I am Snow White," said the princess.

"I'm Doc," said the dwarf
with the eyeglasses.
He seemed to be
the leader.

"I'm Happy,"
said the little man
with the big smile.

"And my name is Grumpy,"
said the one with the grouchy face.

"I'm Bashful," said the fourth dwarf.
He did not look at Snow White.
He was twisting his beard.

"I'm Sneezy,
said the next one
between sneezes.

"My name is Sleepy,"
said the sixth dwarf.
"And that's Dopey,"
he added, pointing
to the little man
beside Snow White.
"He never says anything."

The seven dwarfs took Snow White
downstairs. It was getting late, and they
were very hungry.

Snow White cooked supper for everybody.
It was easy with so many people to help.

"This is the best food I ever ate," said
Happy.

Even Grumpy did not look as grumpy as
usual. It was just like having a party
with Snow White at the table.

Later that night, the dwarfs sat in a circle
around Snow White.

The princess told the little men
about the wicked queen
who wanted to kill her.

"Oh, Snow White, you MUST stay here
and live with us," said Doc.
"We will hide you from the queen."

The next morning the dwarfs went off to work.
Snow White waved good-by to them.

"Don't let anyone in," Doc told her.
"The queen may be looking for you."

But the queen was not looking for Snow White.
She was looking into her magic mirror.

"Mirror, mirror on the wall. Now, who's the
fairest one of all?" she asked.

The mirror answered, "In the house
of the seven dwarfs, Snow White still lives.
SHE is the fairest one of all."

"Snow White still lives?" cried the angry queen.
"We'll see about that!"

She rushed down the steep and winding stairs
to a secret room under the castle wall.

In that dark place,
the queen grabbed
a dusty bottle
from the shelf.

She took a long drink
from the old bottle.

Poof!
She turned into
an ugly witch.

Then the witch took two more bottles—
a green bottle and a red one—.
She poured them into a big iron pot.
She was making a magic brew.

Next the old witch dipped an apple into the pot.
"One taste of this," she said, "and Snow White's
eyes will close forever."

The witch took the magic apple to the house
of the seven dwarfs. There she found Snow White,
with her animal friends.

"All alone, my pet?" said the wicked witch.
"Here. Take one of my lovely apples."

"Thank you," said Snow White.
And she took a big bite.

Suddenly she fell to the ground.
Her eyes were closed as if in a deep sleep.

"Ha!" cried the wicked witch. "My spell
has worked. Snow White sleeps.

I hope she sleeps forever!"

The queen did not see
all the animals running
off into the woods.

The animals ran to the cave of the seven dwarfs.

"Something is wrong!" said Doc.

"Snow White must be in trouble," said Happy.

The seven dwarfs raced home to help the princess.

The wicked witch saw the dwarfs coming.
She began to run. She ran so fast
she didn't look where she was going.
And that was the end of her!

The dwarfs found Snow White in a deep sleep.
"Wake up!" said Doc, tugging at her hand.
"Wake up! Please wake up!" cried the others.

But no matter what they did, they could not
wake the princess.

The dwarfs made a beautiful golden bed:
They put Snow White on it.
Day after day they watched over her.
Day after day they placed flowers on her.
And still the princess slept.

Time passed. . . .

Then one day a prince came riding his horse into the woods. He had heard of the princess who lay sleeping there on her golden bed.

The handsome prince found the sleeping princess. He saw that she was more beautiful than the flowers around her bed. He bent down and kissed her.

Snow White opened her eyes.
At last the wicked spell was broken.
She sat up, smiling at the handsome prince.

How the dwarfs cheered! How they laughed
and danced and sang!

The prince put Snow White on his horse and
carried her off to his castle. There they were
married and lived happily ever after. And the
seven dwarfs came often to visit at their castle.

Sleepy

Bashful

Dopey